HOW TO BUILD JAY

THE LEGO® NINJAGO® MOVIE™
OFFICIAL ANNUAL 2018

TABLE OF CONTENTS

ALMOST CONQUERORS

UNDER GARMADON'S COMMAND, THE SHARK ARMY HAS SET OUT TO CONQUER NINJAGO CITY! BUT THEY'VE BEEN BEATEN BY THE NINJA AND THEY HAVE TO FLEE FOR THE THIRD TIME THIS WEEK! LOOK AT THE SHARK WARRIORS HIDING IN THE DEBRIS AND MATCH THEM INTO PAIRS. THEN COUNT ALL THE LOST WEAPONS.

SECRET NINJA FORCE

HERE ARE THE NINJA – THE PROTECTORS OF NINJAGO CITY: KAI, LLOYD, NYA, COLE, JAY AND ZANE. CAN YOU FIND THEIR NAMES IN THE WORD SEARCH PUZZLE ON THE WALL?

```
L L A D J A Z Y
L K L H A H A M
J L L O Y D N P
E M O C O L E L
K N Y A H O P L
A M A S K A I O
L L O K N Y E M
```

FISHCHAKU
INVENT THE NAMES OF THE WEAPONS USED BY THE ARMY, AND WRITE THEM IN THE BOXES.

UNMASKED

The secret ninja force is defending Ninjago City from Garmadon's army! Match the ninja to their everyday style portraits. Then find the ninja who appears twice.

13

FOUR AGAINST ONE!

A SURVEILLANCE CAMERA HAS CAPTURED LLOYD'S FIGHT WITH FOUR SHARK WARRIORS. WHAT HAS CHANGED MOMENTS LATER? CIRCLE THE EIGHT DIFFERENCES IN THE SECOND PICTURE.

JAY HAS TAKEN OFF IN HIS FIGHTER PLANE. WHICH HIGHLIGHTED ELEMENTS DON'T MATCH THE PICTURE?

THERE ARE NINE OF GARMADON'S WARRIORS HIDDEN SOMEWHERE AROUND HERE. BUT WHERE ARE THEY?

COLE'S ATTACK

COLE'S MECH IS CHARGING LIKE A BATTERING RAM AND BLASTING COOL MUSIC! CAN YOU FIND FOUR SHARK ARMY WEAPONS, TWO HELMETS AND ONE VERY SURPRISED CHICKEN IN THE STORM OF BRICKS?

A WEAPON FOR A NINJA

COLE IS LAUNCHING AN ATTACK, BUT IT SEEMS HE'S MISSING SOMETHING IMPORTANT.

HEY! WHERE'S MY WEAPON? CONNECT THE DOTS AND I'LL BE READY TO FIGHT!

AIM ... FIRE!

NYA IS BOMBARDING THE SHARK ARMY. COUNT HOW MANY OPPONENTS SHE HAS AND TRY TO REMEMBER WHERE THEY ARE. THEN, PLACE THE TIP OF A PENCIL ON THE BARREL OF THE NINJA WARRIOR'S SPIDER VEHICLE. CLOSE YOUR EYES AND USE THE PENCIL TO TRY TO KNOCK OVER AS MANY OF HER OPPONENTS AS POSSIBLE.

DON'T MESS WITH NINJA!

KAI HAS THROWN THE SHARK ARMY WARRIORS THROUGH THE WALL. LOOK AT THE SPRAY PAINTED PORTRAITS OF HIS OPPONENTS AND MATCH EACH OF THEM TO THE CORRECT HOLE.

LURKING IN THE SHADOWS

MATCH THE NINJA SHADOWS TO THEIR STATEMENTS. THEN, COLOUR THE DOT BELOW EACH STATEMENT IN THE CORRECT NINJA'S COLOUR.

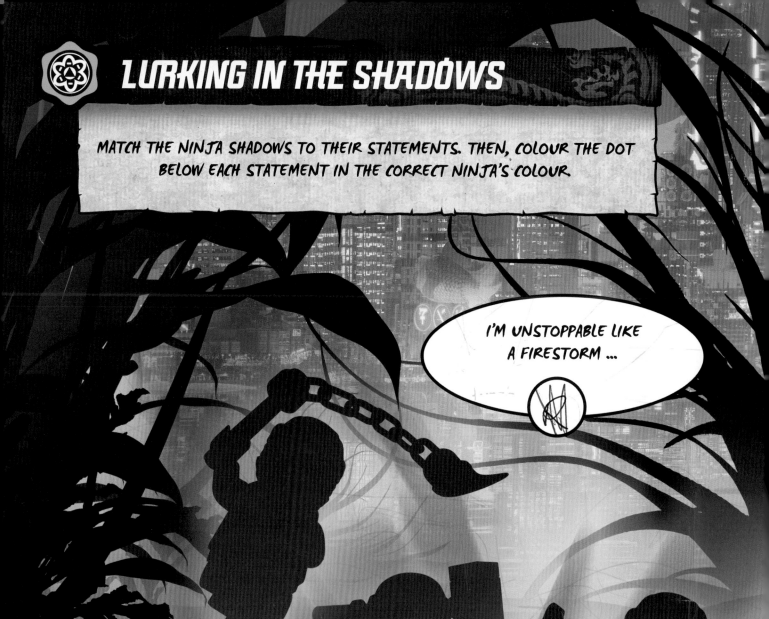

I'M UNSTOPPABLE LIKE A FIRESTORM ...

I FIGHT WITH A HAMMER BECAUSE IT'S HEAVY AND SOLID LIKE THE EARTH.

I STRIVE FOR PERFECTION EVERY DAY!

BLACK NINJA

WHITE NINJA

SILVER NINJA

RED NINJA

BLUE NINJA

GREEN NINJA

I'M LIKE WATER – I CAN BE REALLY NICE AND INCREDIBLY DANGEROUS AT THE SAME TIME!

I STRIKE LIKE LIGHTNING – AT TREMENDOUS SPEED AND WITH A GREAT RUMBLE!

ICE IS HARD, COLD AND SHARP JUST LIKE I AM WITH MY ENEMIES.

TRAINING WITH MASTER WU

USE JAY'S MINIFIGURE AND A DIE TO FIND OUT HOW HE PERFORMED DURING HIS TRAINING WITH MASTER WU TODAY.

YOU FALL INTO DEEP WATER – MOVE BACK ONE SPACE.

BADLY DONE SOMERSAULT – MOVE BACK THREE SPACES.

SUPER PUNCH! MOVE FORWARD TWO SPACES.

START

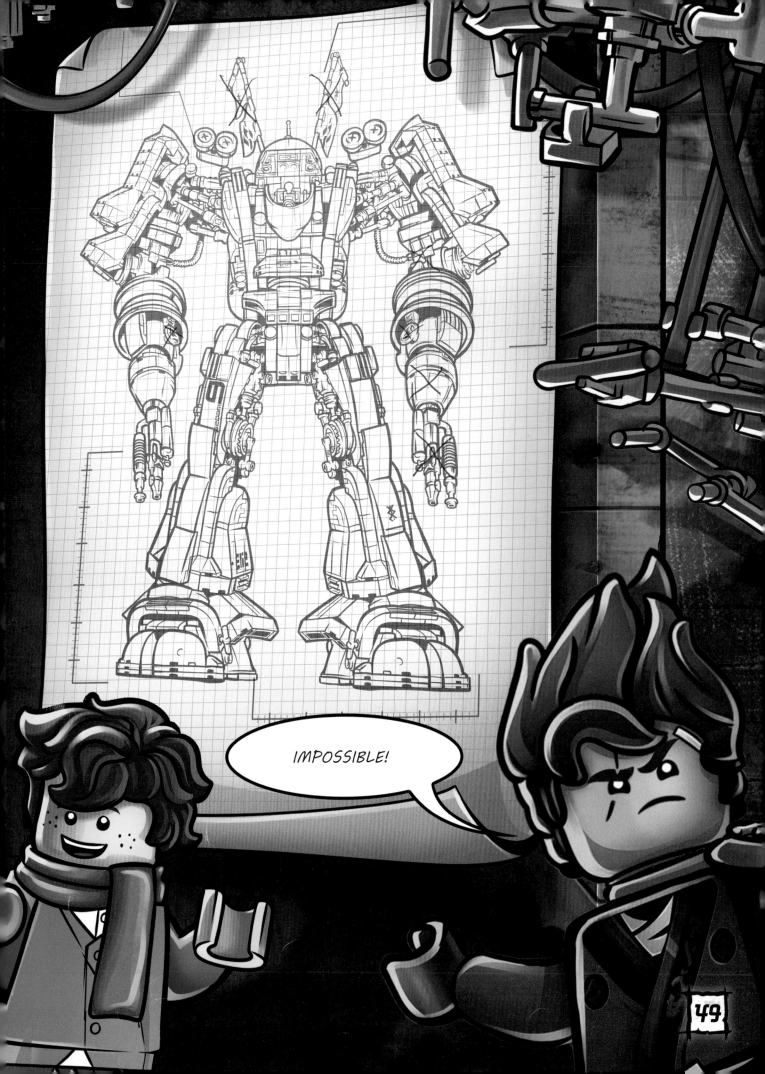

51

ONCE YOU'VE FOUND THEM LOOK FOR SEVEN SWORDS.

WHERE ARE THE NINJA?

GARMADON'S SHARK MECH IS FIGHTING THE NINJA. FIND THE NINJA WHO APPEARS TWICE ON THE PAGE AND CIRCLE THEIR PORTRAIT. THEN MARK THE NINJA WHO IS ABSENT FROM THE BATTLE.

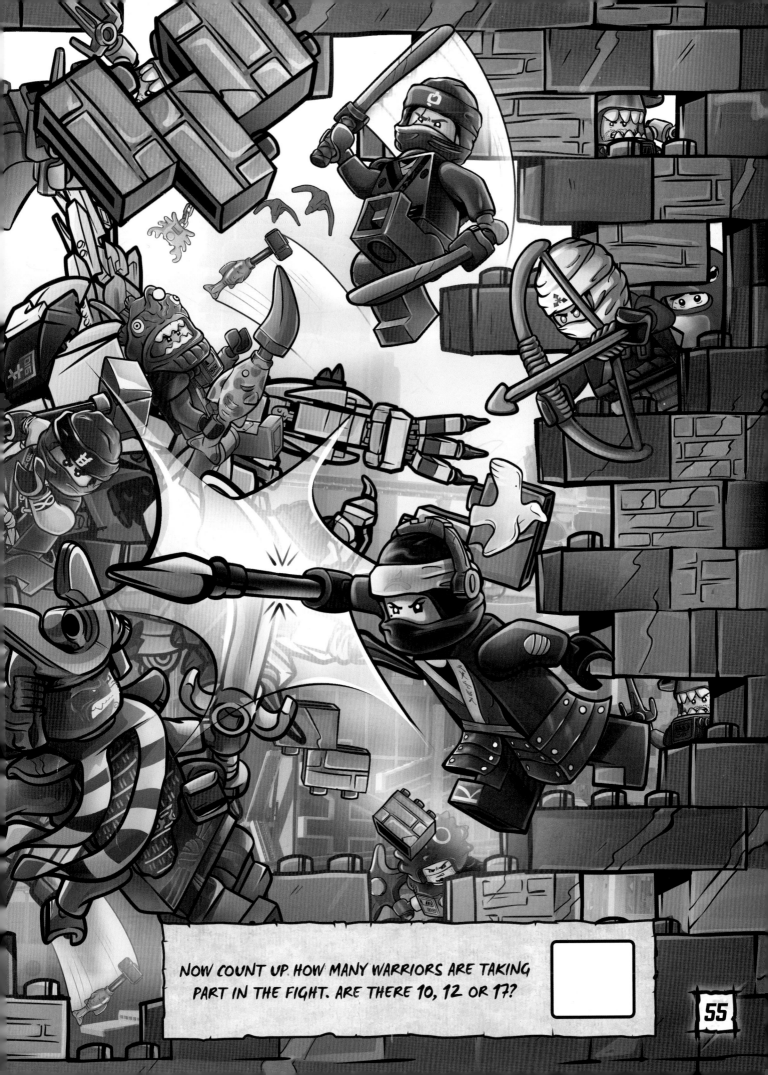

NOW COUNT UP. HOW MANY WARRIORS ARE TAKING PART IN THE FIGHT. ARE THERE 10, 12 OR 17?

LOST WEAPON

LOOK AT THE WEAPONS THIS WARRIOR IS THINKING ABOUT. FIND THEM ALL IN THE PICTURE AND WRITE DOWN HOW MANY OF EACH KIND THERE ARE.

ANSWERS

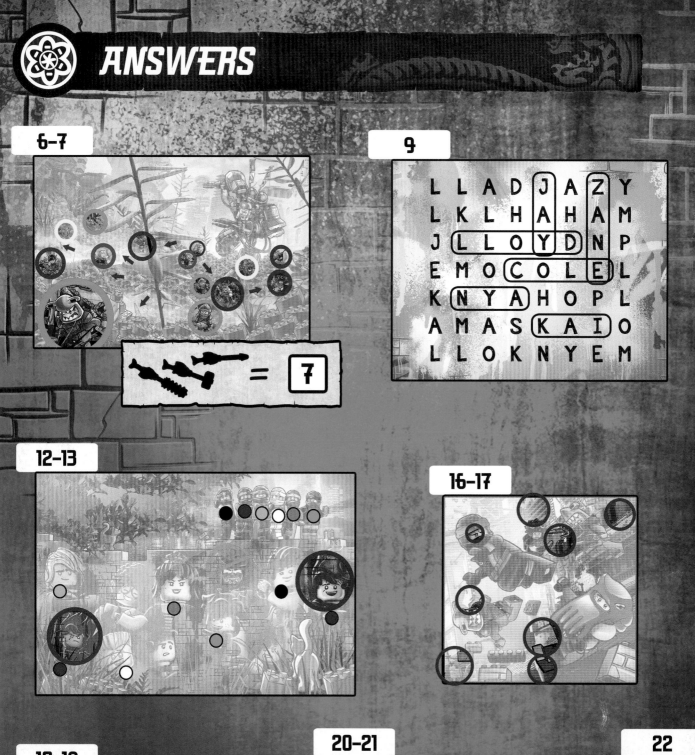

6-7

9

L	L	A	D	J	A	Z	Y
L	K	L	H	A	H	A	M
J	L	L	O	Y	D	N	P
E	M	O	C	O	L	E	L
K	N	Y	A	H	O	P	L
A	M	A	S	K	A	I	O
L	L	O	K	N	Y	E	M

= **7**

12-13

16-17

18-19

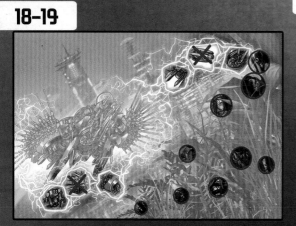

20-21

22

6

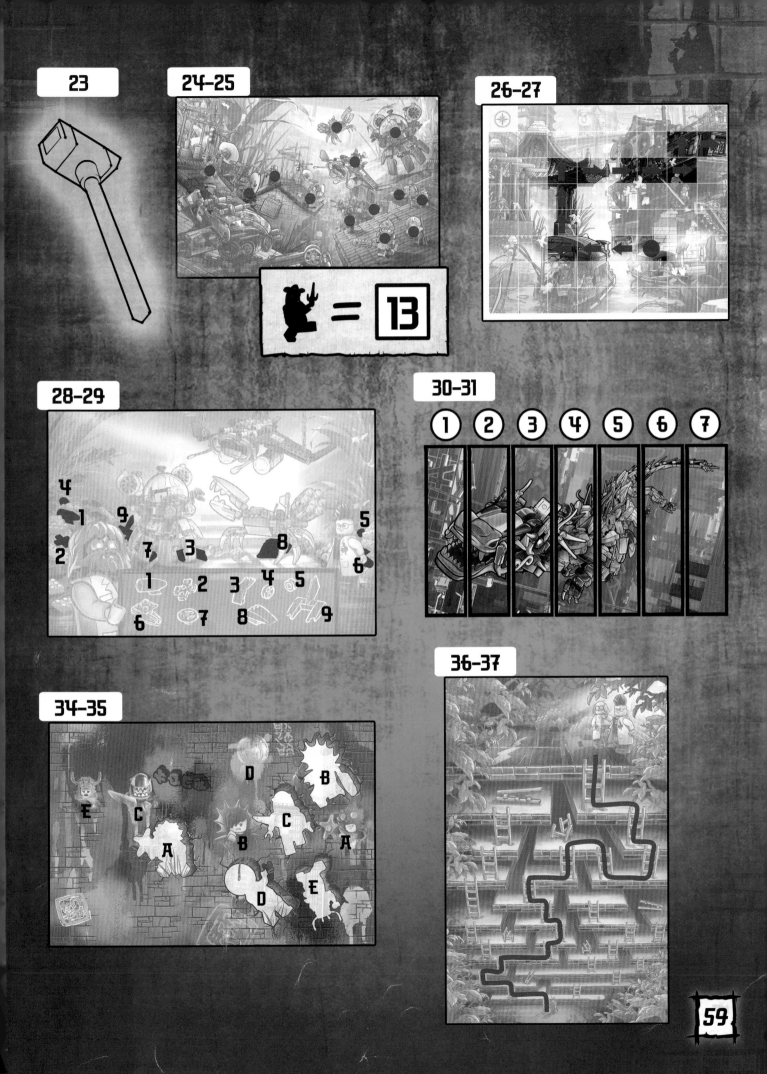

23

24-25

26-27

= 13

28-29

4
1   9
2   7   3   8
          5
          6
1   2   3   4   5
6   7   8   9

30-31

① ② ③ ④ ⑤ ⑥ ⑦

34-35

D   B
E   C   C
A   A
B
D   E

36-37

38-39

42-43

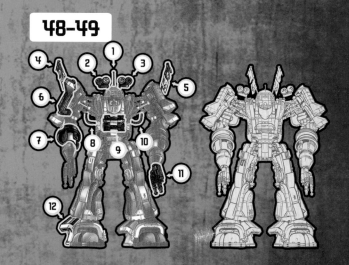

46-47

48-49

50-51

52-53

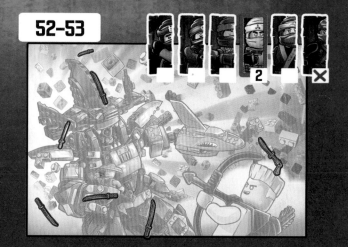

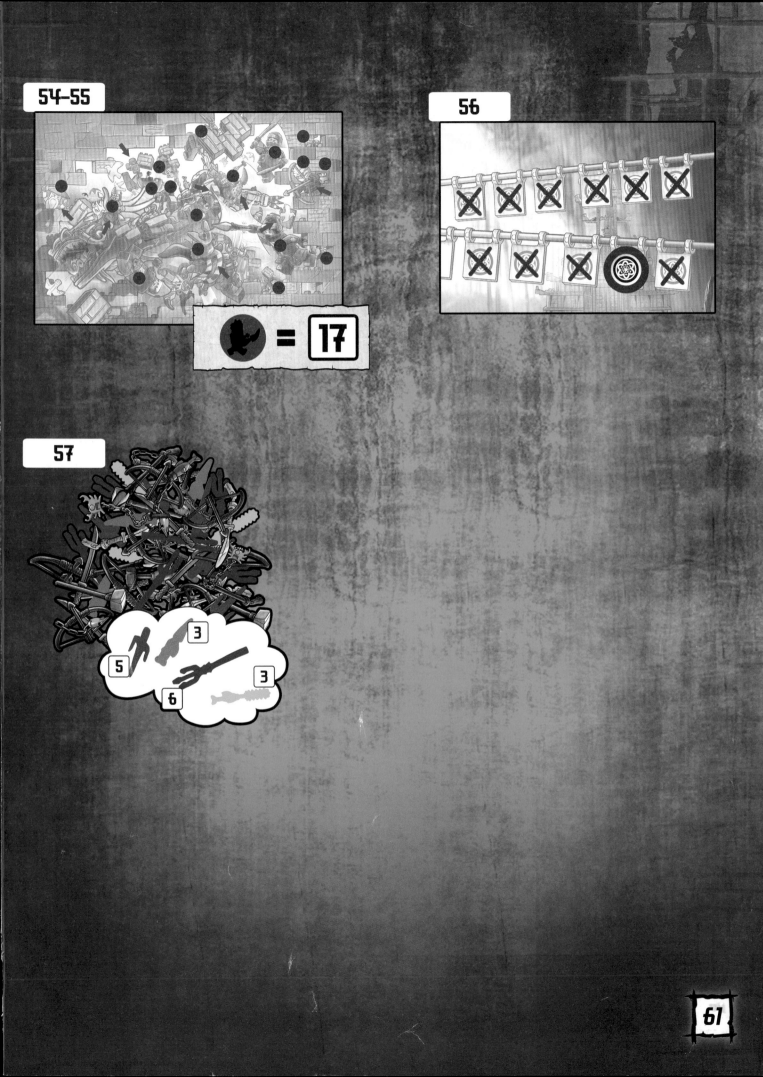

54–55

56

● = **17**

57

5 3 6 3